DUCKLING DIARY

Also in the Animal Ark Pets series

LUCY DANIELS
Duckling
Diary

Illustrated by Paul Howard

Hodder
Children's
Books

a division of Hodder Headline plc

Special thanks to Sue Welford

First published in Great Britain in 1998
by Hodder Children's Books

A Catalogue record for this book is available from the British Library

ISBN 0 340 71372 0

Typeset by Avon Dataset Ltd, Bidford-on-Avon, Warks

Printed and bound in Great Britain by
Mackays of Chatham plc, Chatham, Kent

Hodder Children's Books
a division of Hodder Headline plc
338 Euston Road
London NW1 3BH

Contents

1

An exciting discovery

"There she is!" Mandy Hope whispered excitedly. "She's coming back."

Mandy and her best friend, James Hunter, were lying on their stomachs in the long grass overlooking Millers Pond.

James's young Labrador, Blackie, was with them.

They were all watching a mallard's nest. The mother duck had left it for a few minutes to feed, but now she had returned.

Mandy and James had been watching the duck for weeks now. First they had seen her building her nest. She had gathered sticks and reeds and woven them into a beautiful nest on a small island just off the bank. Then she had laid her eggs, sitting on them patiently to keep them warm, and quietly waiting for them to hatch.

Today was the first time Mandy and James had been able to see just how many eggs lay snugly in the nest. There were five and Mandy was delighted.

"Five eggs!" she whispered. "Five babies! Ooh, James, I just can't wait."

Mandy had been studying the duck for a project her class was doing at school. When Mrs Todd had first told the class that they were each going to study an animal or bird for a class project, Mandy had to think really hard.

She knew her classmates with pets would study their own animals. They'd all come up with ideas straight away. One boy was going to call his study, *Gerbil Journal*, another's was going to be called *Rabbit Record*, while someone else was writing a *Hamster History*. Mandy didn't want to do the same as someone else. But she wasn't left with much to choose from. Then she and James had discovered the mallard's nest and her problem was solved. Hers would be *Duckling Diary*!

After every visit, Mandy had written down her progress in her project book. When the ducklings were hatched, she intended to keep a record of *them* as well.

Now they watched the duck settle down. She preened herself for a little while, then sat contentedly. The bright spring sunshine warmed her gleaming pale brown feathers.

James gave a sigh. "I wonder when they're going to hatch? It seems as if she's been sitting there forever."

"I know," Mandy said. "I hope it's soon."

"Come on," James whispered. "We'd better go before she spots us."

Mandy didn't want to leave, but she knew they must not disturb the duck. Lying there in the grass, the sun shining and the bees buzzing from wild flower to wild flower, Mandy felt as if she was in heaven.

James was right, though. It was great to watch wildlife, but you had to be careful not to interfere.

So they crept quietly away.

James held tightly to Blackie's lead. The last thing they wanted was for Blackie to have one of his bursts of energy and go charging around.

The sky was a deep vivid blue as Mandy and James ran along the field's edge and out into the lane to make their way home.

They both lived in the village of Welford, where Mandy's parents were the local vets. Their surgery was attached to a stone-built cottage where the family lived. The surgery was called Animal Ark.

As they were going by the village green, Mandy suddenly realised there wasn't much point in going home just yet. Her mum would be taking a busy small-animal surgery this time of day and her dad would be out on his calls. "*I* know!" she said suddenly.

"What?" James stopped beside her. He pushed his glasses back up on his nose and jerked Blackie away from a cat that had innocently crossed his path.

"Why don't we go to Lilac Cottage and tell Gran and Grandad?" Mandy suggested.

"Tell them what?"

"About the five eggs, silly. Don't you think it's a good idea?"

James nodded. "You bet."

Visiting Mandy's grandparents was always a good idea. Mandy's gran made the best biscuits and lemonade in the whole world.

"Come on," he added. "Race you!"

Mandy laughed out loud as James set off. His legs were going like pistons as Blackie pulled him as fast as could be.

"It's not fair," she shouted, as he surged on ahead.

James managed to halt the puppy and stood waiting for her, panting. "Sorry." He grinned. "But I could probably still beat you even without Blackie's help."

Mandy grinned back. It was great having a friend like James. Not only did he love animals as much as she did, he also let her share Blackie. She would really have liked to have pets of her own, but knew it was impossible. The family was so busy looking after other people's animals that there just wasn't time to look after any of their own.

She grabbed Blackie's lead from James's hand and ran on ahead, calling over her shoulder. "*Now* let's see who beats who!"

In fact, they arrived at the cottage gate together.

"What on earth's going on!" Gran exclaimed, as they both burst through the back door, giggling and laughing. Blackie flopped down on the floor, panting.

Mandy explained about their race. Then she said excitedly, "Guess what, Gran?"

"Now calm down, Mandy." Gran looked as if she was just about to go out. But however busy she was, she always had time to listen to her granddaughter. "What's all this about?"

"Eggs!" Mandy said.

"Five of them!" added James.

"Eggs?" Gran looked puzzled.

"In the nest," Mandy continued. "You know, the one on Millers Pond."

"Oh . . . the *duck's* nest," Gran said. "Five! My goodness, the mother's going to be busy, isn't she?"

"Busy?" Grandad came in from the garden. "I'm always busy."

Mandy laughed and explained that they weren't talking about him.

Grandad was carrying a basket of spring cabbage from the garden. He had mud all over his shoes. Gran frowned as he came into the kitchen without taking them off. He bent down hurriedly and untied the laces. He gave his wife a grin. "Sorry, Dorothy." He winked at James. "All right, James?"

"Yes, thanks," he replied.

Grandad bent to pat Blackie as Mandy explained about the nest and the pond and the eggs.

"Millers Pond . . ." Grandad smiled. "I used to go there when I was a boy. My pals and I made a raft once. It sank first time. My, did we get into trouble for getting our clothes all wet. I remember—"

Mandy tapped her fingers impatiently. She loved hearing Grandad's stories. But not now. Right now she wanted to know about duck eggs.

"Grandad," she said quickly, "do you know how long duck eggs take to hatch?"

"Um . . . no, I don't, love. Sorry." He plonked the basket on the draining-board and scrubbed his hands under the tap. "Have you got any idea, Dorothy?" he asked Gran.

She shook her head. "No, sorry. Haven't a clue." She glanced at her watch, then dropped a quick kiss on top of Mandy's head. "I must go. My friend Kathy's expecting me. We're organising a Women's Institute visit to that new farm park just outside the village."

"I saw an advert for it in the local paper," James piped up. "It's called Woodbridge Farm Park."

"That's right," Gran said. "It used to be an ordinary farm, but the new owners have turned it into a place where the public can go to see how a farm really works. The WI are having a guided tour and we've got a few more details to fix."

"Are there lots of animals?" Mandy asked.

"I believe so. And poultry. Kathy keeps a lot of chickens, so she'll be especially interested."

"I'll take you and James one day, if you like," Grandad offered.

Mandy's eyes shone. "That would be great, wouldn't it, James?"

"Yes." James was trying not to look glum. His heart had sunk when he saw Mandy's gran was just going out. His vision of home-made biscuits and lemonade was disappearing fast.

Gran must have noticed. "Help yourself to something to eat," she told them, with a twinkle in her eye.

Mandy gave her a swift hug. "Thanks, Gran."

When she had gone, Mandy turned to her grandad. "Won't it be great, Grandad? Five ducklings!"

"Wonderful," he said. He was rummaging in the pantry for the biscuit tin. He found it, opened the lid and put it on the kitchen table in front of them. Blackie sat up hopefully as his nose caught the scent.

"Mind you," Grandad added, "you'd better be sure to keep Blackie under control. Labradors are inclined to chase ducks, you know."

James *did* know. Labradors were inclined to chase anything that moved.

"We will," he promised the old man.

"Good." Grandad opened the fridge door and took out a tall bottle of pale lemonade. "Because she'll desert the nest if she gets scared," he continued.

Mandy looked at James in horror. "We won't let that happen, honestly, Grandad."

When they had washed up their glasses and plates, admired Grandad's spring cabbages and inspected his tomato plants, Mandy and James headed off home.

They split up at the green, as James lived on the other side of the village.

"We'll go back first thing tomorrow, shall we?" Mandy suggested.

"Right," James replied. "And I'll threaten Blackie with no dinner if he doesn't behave himself."

Mandy grinned. "OK, see you tomorrow!"

2

Good boy, Blackie!

The mobile library van was parked by the village green. Peggy, the librarian, was just helping one of Welford's elderly residents down the steps.

"Hi, Mandy," she called, when she saw Mandy hurrying past. "Don't you want any books today?"

Mandy halted. Maybe Peggy had a

book about ducks. She walked across the green and up the van steps. Inside were racks of books and a little desk where Peggy checked people's tickets and stamped the books with the date they had to be returned.

"Have you got any about ducks, please?" Mandy asked.

Peggy went to look on the shelves and came back with a book: *All You Need to Know About Ducks*. She handed it to Mandy.

It was exactly what Mandy wanted. "Oh, that's great. Thanks, Peggy." Then her face fell. "Oh . . . I haven't got my ticket with me."

Peggy smiled. "Never mind. I'll look your number up on the computer when I get back to Walton Library." She stamped the inside of the book. "So why do you want a book about ducks?"

Mandy explained.

"*Five* eggs. How wonderful!" Peggy said. "Well, good luck with the duck-lings."

"Thanks." Mandy tucked the book under her arm and set off for home again.

Back at Animal Ark, Mandy's mum had just finished morning surgery. She was in the kitchen, sitting with her feet up on a chair and drinking a cup of coffee when Mandy came in.

"What a morning!" she said to Mandy with a sigh. "Five cats, three dogs, a budgie, a gerbil and a lizard."

"A lizard!" Mandy exclaimed. "That's unusual."

"Yes. Tommy Day, from that house next to the post office, he found a lizard without a tail on his garden wall. He was really worried, but I assured him it would grow a new one."

Mandy was brimming with her own news. She told her mum about the eggs all in a rush, and showed her the book she had borrowed from the library van.

"Excellent," Mrs Hope said. "You'll have to be very careful not to disturb the mother."

"Oh, we will be," Mandy said. "We *are* being very careful already."

"That's good, then." Mandy's mum got up and put her cup into the dishwasher. "Well, love, duty calls. I'll see you later." She planted a swift kiss on top of Mandy's head. "Dad's in the surgery if you need him." She picked up her bag and went out.

Mandy went upstairs to her room to lie on her bed and study the duck book. When it came to the page that told you about hatching out eggs, she drew in her breath. She ran to her desk to check her project book.

It had been almost six weeks since she and James had first spotted the duck building her nest. Two weeks to build it . . . four weeks to sit on the eggs. She looked at the dates, carefully written down since that first day. Her heart leaped with excitement as she worked it out.

She ran downstairs to the phone and quickly dialled James's number.

"James," she said, before he'd hardly

had a chance to say hello. "The eggs. They're due to hatch tomorrow!"

"Tomorrow!" James said. "That'll be brilliant."

"Come over as early as you can."

"I will. Definitely."

The following morning, Mandy was up bright and early. The warm mist promised another fine spring day. She waited anxiously at the gate for James, and soon spotted him rushing down the lane, Blackie bounding on ahead.

"Won't it be great if the eggs really do hatch today?" James's voice was full of excitement.

"Brilliant!" Mandy said. "My book said incubation varies from twenty-eight to thirty days. Today's the twenty-eighth day, I'm sure. So let's keep our fingers crossed."

But, as they approached the pond, they suddenly heard a terrible, frantic quacking and a splashing of water. Then a beating of wings. They looked up to see a duck

fly up and away towards the cornfield, quacking in terror.

Mandy looked at James in horror. "That's our duck, I'm sure!" she cried. "Quick!"

They ran as fast as they could through the long grass towards the pond.

When they got to the water's edge, a terrible scene met their eyes. Mandy's hand flew to her mouth and she stood there in stunned silence.

"Oh, no!" James exclaimed.

The little bank-side island was empty.

It *was* the mother duck they had seen. Her nest had been destroyed and she had flown away. There was no sign of the eggs. All that was left were reeds and twigs floating round the island in sad little bundles.

"Poor duck!" Mandy wailed. "Now what's she going to do?" Tears rolled down her cheeks.

Blackie came and licked her hand. He always seemed to know when people were upset.

James was almost crying too. "Who could have done it?" he asked, shaking his head.

Suddenly, Blackie bounded off towards the little island. There didn't seem to be much point in going after him. The duck had been frightened away already. Blackie sniffed around in the long grass for a minute, then came trotting back.

Mandy was still sobbing.

"I bet it was a fox," James said.

"Yes," Mandy agreed tearfully. "I know foxes have to eat, but why did it have to be our duck eggs?"

Blackie nudged Mandy's knee. He had placed something on the grass in front of her. It was an egg; a duck's egg. A perfect, *unbroken* duck's egg.

Forgetting her tears, Mandy picked it up and cradled it gently in her hands. It was still warm! "Oh, James."

He stared at the egg, then gave Blackie a big hug. "Good boy, Blackie!"

"James," Mandy said urgently, "do you remember when Libby Masters' pet hen Ronda was hatching out her chicks? Ronda could only leave the eggs for a few minutes, otherwise they would get cold and the chicks inside would have died."

James nodded. "Right. So we've got to keep this egg warm and get it somewhere where it will *stay* warm – and as quickly as we can, so the baby duck inside doesn't die."

"Gran and Grandad are nearest," Mandy suggested.

"Right," James replied. "Come on!"

With Mandy holding the egg in both hands, close to her body for warmth, they hurried towards Lilac Cottage.

Grandad was surprised to see the three of them so early in the day, although he had been up for a long time. He was in his greenhouse tying up his budding tomato plants with a web of string to support them. Gran had just gone out shopping.

"What on earth's wrong?" Grandad asked, when he saw their anxious faces.

"Oh, Grandad!" Mandy quickly told him what had happened. "Where can we put the egg to keep it warm?"

"Right! The airing cupboard should do for the time being," Grandad replied.

They all hurried indoors. Mandy walked carefully up the stairs and placed the egg on a bundle of Gran's snowy-white towels on the shelf nearest the hot-water tank.

"That should do it," she murmured. She touched the shell gently with her

22

fingertip. "Now you keep nice and warm, baby duck. We're going to look after you, so you needn't worry." Mandy closed the airing-cupboard door softly and ran back downstairs.

Grandad and James were sitting at the kitchen table.

"Well," Grandad said. "*Now* what are you going to do?"

3

Keeping warm

Mandy shook her head. She knew that the egg had to be kept at the right temperature for it to hatch, but without a mother bird to do the job, how was she going to manage it?

"Why don't we call Libby Masters' dad?" James suggested. "He keeps chickens, but he might know about ducks as well."

"Brilliant, James!" Mandy replied. "Let's do it straight away! Can we, Grandad?"

"Of course, love," her grandad replied. "The number should be in the phone book."

Mandy hurried into the hall, then found and dialled the number for Blackheath Farm. But it rang and rang. No one was in. She sighed, and went back into the kitchen. "No answer," she told them, unhappily.

Then Mandy's face suddenly lit up. "*I* know!" she said. "Gran's friend Kathy! Gran told us she kept chickens, so *she* might be able to tell us what to do next."

"Good thinking," Grandad said. "I'll go and have a word with her for you."

He seemed to be on the phone for ages. "Yes . . . No . . . Oh, dear . . . I am sorry . . . Yes, I'm sure you will . . . Was he? Oh, what a shame . . . But he lived a normal life? . . . Oh, yes, that's good . . ."

James looked at Mandy. "What are they talking about?"

Mandy shrugged. "I don't know, but

it doesn't sound like ducks to me."

After a few more minutes, Grandad called out. "Kathy wants to know when you think the egg is due to hatch."

"Today," Mandy said urgently. "We think it could well be today."

Eventually, Grandad came back into the kitchen. "That woman," he said. "She certainly knows how to talk! She's been telling me all about her poor cat."

"What's wrong with it?" James asked.

"It died, poor thing. She's very upset."

"Oh dear," Mandy murmured. She felt sad that Kathy's cat had died, but she was desperate to know what Kathy had said about the egg. She wriggled impatiently in her chair. "Grandad, what did she say about the—"

"The egg? Oh, yes. Right." He opened one of the kitchen cupboards and took out a large glass mixing bowl. "This'll do."

"Won't Gran mind?" Mandy asked anxiously.

"Not if it's in a good cause." Grandad

grinned. "You know Gran's always in favour of good causes. Come on. Follow me and I'll show you what we're going to do."

First, Grandad went down to his compost heap and filled the bottom of the bowl with grass cuttings. They were still damp from the dew, and warm from the early morning sun. Then he took it into the greenhouse.

"Kathy said the egg needs to be kept warm and slightly damp." He made a small hollow in the grass cuttings, then he put the bowl on the floor. He took his greenhouse heater, placed it near the bowl, and plugged it in.

"Kathy said the egg has to be kept at a certain constant temperature." He set the dial on the heater. "Right, Mandy, go and fetch the egg."

Mandy ran indoors and up the stairs. She took the egg out gently and walked carefully back downstairs and out to the greenhouse.

Grandad took it from her and placed it

in the warm nest. Then he covered the bowl with a dark cloth, and turned to Mandy and James. "Now," he said, "all we have to do is wait."

"What for?" came a voice from the doorway.

Mandy turned to see Gran standing there. She ran towards her. "Oh, Gran, you'll never guess what."

Mandy told her what had happened. "Oh dear. Poor duck," Gran said, then gazed at Grandad. "But Kathy said it

would be quite easy to hatch this egg out?"

"Should be," Grandad confirmed.

"In my best mixing bowl?"

Grandad looked a bit sheepish.

"Oh, Gran, you don't mind, do you?" Mandy cried.

Gran smiled. "No, of course not."

Mandy clapped her hands together. "Oh, Gran. Won't it be brilliant?"

"It certainly will." She patted Mandy's arm. "You and James go and start unloading the shopping from the car. There's a good girl."

"OK." Mandy's eyes were still shining. "Come on, James."

By the time Mandy and James had unloaded the shopping, Gran and Grandad were back in the kitchen.

"They had kept it warm but it had been pretty shaken up," Grandad was saying. "All we can do is wait and keep our fingers crossed."

"Oh dear," Mandy heard Gran say. "They'll be so upset if nothing happens."

Mandy's heart turned over. By the look on Grandad's face, he thought the egg might not hatch out.

She had to go and look at it, just to make sure it was all right. But Gran caught her arm as she went past. "A watched pot never boils," she told her. "If you keep going to look, it will seem ages before it hatches. Best leave it alone, Mandy. Just let nature take its course."

Mandy sighed and sat down reluctantly. Gran put the kettle on for a cup of tea and then began to unpack the bags and put the shopping away. James was helping. Grandad began telling Gran about Kathy's cat.

"Oh dear," Gran said. "The old boy did look as if he was on his last legs when I last visited Kathy. She'll miss him terribly. He was deaf, you know."

"Poor thing," James said.

Gran smiled. "Oh, Snowball led a great life. And the beauty was, he couldn't hear Kathy's chicks cheeping, so he didn't try to chase them. He was really the perfect cat for her."

Mandy leaned her chin on her hands and stared out of the window. She could just see the greenhouse from where she was sitting. "You *will* let me know as soon as anything happens, won't you?" she asked her grandparents anxiously.

"Of course!" Grandad said.

"Even if it's in the middle of the night?"

Gran laughed. "We don't mind keeping your egg for you, you two. But we're not staying up all night, I'm afraid. Not even for a duckling."

Mandy managed a grin. "I know. But you could look first thing in the morning."

Gran poured boiling water into the teapot. "Knowing you, Mandy, you'll be here before your grandad and I are even out of bed."

"And me," James said, eyeing the biscuit tin.

"Yes, James," Gran said. "And you."

Before they left, Mandy couldn't resist having just one more peep at the egg. If there was a crack in the shell it would mean the duckling was starting to peck its way out.

But the egg lay there in the bowl, still perfect, not a crack to be seen. She touched the delicate shell with the tip of her finger. There was a picture of an unborn duckling in the book she'd got from the library van. It was all curled up tight; so big it filled the whole of the inside of the egg. Mandy could just imagine this one, curled round, eyes closed, resting before it was ready to face the big wide world.

"Please be all right," she whispered, as she touched the egg again. "Please be all right."

As she spoke, the egg moved. Just a tiny bit, wobbling from side to side. Mandy blinked. Had she imagined it? She touched it again. Maybe her finger had disturbed it. But it didn't wobble again. It just lay there, warm and still.

Mandy sighed. James was waiting with Blackie at the gate. She put the dark cloth back over the top, went out and closed the door softly behind her. Gran was right again – a watched pot never boils.

4

Crossing bridges

Mr Hope was out on a call when Mandy arrived back at Animal Ark, bursting with good and bad duck news. Mrs Hope was in the waiting-room pinning a notice to the board.

"I'm sorry, love," she said, as she heard what had happened. "That kind of thing often happens in nature."

"I know," Mandy said. "But at least we might be able to save one of the baby ducks."

Her mum gave her a quick hug. "Yes, although I'm not sure what you'll do with it if it does hatch."

Mandy didn't really want to think about that yet. "We'll cross that bridge when we come to it," was another of Gran's favourite sayings. And that's what Mandy had decided to do.

She ran upstairs to update her project book before lunch. She wiped a tear from her eye as she wrote about the nest being destroyed. She hoped her friends wouldn't have such sad things to write about in *their* project books.

When she had finished she looked at her library book again. At the end was a chapter about newly hatched ducklings.

"'When it hatches, a duckling will imprint on the first thing it sees,'" Mandy read. She wasn't quite sure what "imprint" meant, but made up her mind to ask her mum at lunch. On the same page there was a picture of a long line of fluffy yellow ducklings waddling confidently along behind their mother.

Mandy closed the book and sighed. What was her poor duckling going to do without a mother to follow?

Mrs Hope was getting lunch as Mandy ran downstairs and into the kitchen. "Imprint?" she said, when Mandy asked her. "It means that the first thing a duckling sees will stay in its mind and it will follow that thing everywhere. That's usually its mum, of course. It's nature's way of keeping some young creatures safe."

"Oh . . ." Mandy had started laying the table. Now she stopped, fiddling with a fork and staring into space.

Mrs Hope could see something was wrong. "What's worrying you, love?" she asked gently.

Mandy sighed. "Our duckling won't have a mother to imprint upon." She looked at her mum with tears in her eyes. "Poor little thing."

Mrs Hope smiled reassuringly. "Oh, Mandy, you know what Gran says about crossing bridges."

"Yes." Mandy sniffed.

"Well, let's do that, shall we? Your baby duck will be safe. That's really all that matters."

Mandy brightened. "Yes, I suppose so."

The following morning Mandy was up two hours before it was time to leave for school. She'd made her sandwiches and had just finished eating her cereal when Mr Hope came into the kitchen.

"You're up early, Mandy," he remarked.

She explained about going to check if the egg had hatched. Then her mum came in.

"You're up early," she said, and Mandy had to explain all over again.

"They'll probably still be in bed," she heard her mum say to her dad as she grabbed her schoolbag and hurried out.

It was another lovely morning. The sun had risen above an early mist and the dew on the village green sparkled like diamonds. Mandy felt full of hope as she cycled down the lane and turned into the sleepy village street towards Lilac Cottage.

She left her bike by the gate. There was no sign of Gran or Grandad as she hurried up the garden path. Round the back, the greenhouse door was closed.

Mandy's heart thumped as she opened it and went inside. She stood and stared at the bowl for a second or two. Then, hardly daring to breathe, she reached down and carefully lifted off the cover.

"Oh . . . !" Mandy's heart thudded with excitement. The egg had cracked in half, and there, in the centre, was a tiny, beautiful, fluffy, browny-yellow duckling.

The duckling lay in the grass cuttings, tired from its hard job of pecking through the eggshell. It stirred and shook its little head, then opened its bright beady eyes.

"Ohhh." Mandy breathed again. "Hello, little one." She stretched out her fingertip and gently touched its downy head. It cheeped softly, dark eyes staring at her through the glass. "Welcome to Welford," Mandy said softly.

She heard a sound behind her and turned to see Grandad standing in the doorway.

"Come and see, Grandad!"

He crouched down beside her. "Well, hello, little thing."

Mandy's eyes were shining as she looked at him. "You *are* clever, Grandad."

He grinned. "Blackie's the clever one really."

"Yes." Mandy gazed back at the duckling. "I'm going to call her Dilly," she said.

As she said the name, the duckling shook itself and got to its feet, cheeping loudly.

"It said in my book that ducklings don't need food for a while after they've hatched," Mandy said. "But she sounds pretty hungry to me."

"I wonder what ducklings eat," Grandad said.

"Wild ducklings eat waterweed and things they find in the pond." Mandy told him. "I'll call for James and we'll go and get some."

"What about school?" Grandad asked.

"Oh . . . well . . . after school."

By now, Gran had arrived to see the new baby. "Isn't she cute!" She bent down beside Mandy and Grandad. "I thought she'd be yellow all over."

"So did I," Mandy said. "But I suppose her mum was brown, so she has some brown on her too."

"That would be it," Grandad said. He stood up. "But you can't always be going off to the pond to find food for her, Mandy." He turned to Gran. "Why don't you give Kathy a ring, Dorothy? She might be able to suggest something else we could give her to eat."

"It's a bit early," Gran replied, still gazing at Dilly. "She'll be out feeding her chickens. I'll call Kathy later and let you know after school, Mandy. I'm sure Dilly will be all right until then."

Mandy could hardly bear to leave. "You will keep an eye on her for me, won't you?" she begged.

Gran gave her a quick hug. "Of course we will, and I'll get whatever duckling food Kathy suggests."

As Mandy turned to walk away, Dilly gave a loud cheep and tried to climb out of the bowl.

"I'll find her a box now she's hatched," Grandad said. "She'll need something bigger than the bowl."

"Thanks, Grandad. That'll be great." Mandy glanced at her watch. If she hurried, she'd just have time to pop back home to tell Mum and Dad the good news. It would be no good calling for James this early. He never got up until the last minute.

Her heart was singing as she sped off back towards Animal Ark. What a great day!

5

The new arrival

Mandy was so excited, that, as she entered the lane which would take her down to Animal Ark, she almost collided with Della Skilton.

"Hey, careful, Mandy!" Della laughed.

Della was the manager of Westmoor House, a nursing home for old people. She was carrying a young black cat in a basket.

"Oh, sorry!" Mandy panted. She eyed the basket anxiously. "Is Cheeky sick?"

"She's been a bit off-colour, so I'm taking her for a check-up. Nothing serious, I'm sure."

"That's good." Mandy didn't have the time to stop and tell her about Dilly just then. "I'd walk with you, but I'm in a bit of a rush," she explained.

"So I can see," Della smiled. She waved goodbye as Mandy shot on ahead.

At Animal Ark, Mandy pushed open the gate, scooted up the path, dumped her bike against the wall and dashed into the surgery.

The receptionist, Jean Knox, was just taking the cover off her computer. She looked up in surprise as Mandy hurtled through the door. "Mandy! What on earth's the matter?"

"The baby's here," Mandy panted. "Are Mum and Dad both still around?"

"Baby?" Jean looked more surprised than ever. "I didn't know anyone in Welford was having a baby."

Mandy laughed. "Oh, no . . . our duckling, she's hatched."

Jean clapped her hands together. "How wonderful!"

Mrs Hope came through from the back. "Mandy! I thought you'd gone ages ago."

"I did." Mandy's eyes were shining. "Now I'm back to tell you the baby's arrived."

"Baby? Oh, the duckling!" Mrs Hope exclaimed. "That's wonderful. Is it OK?"

"She's beautiful. I'm calling her Dilly."

"Dilly?" Her dad came out from the store cupboard carrying a new box of vaccine. "Supposing it's a boy? He won't be pleased to have a name like Dilly."

Mandy looked indignant. "It can be short for Dillon," she said. "There's a boy in our class called Dillon. Actually he's a bit of a bully, but I'm sure Dilly won't be like that with other ducks."

"That's OK, then," Mr Hope said. "Dilly it is."

Everyone burst out laughing, and Mandy knew from the twinkle in her

dad's eye that he was only teasing.

Just then Della arrived with the kitten. Then someone else turned up with a rabbit in a cardboard box. Surgery had started and it was time for Mandy to be off.

"I'm going to see Dilly after school," she called, as Mr and Mrs Hope went through to the back to begin the day's work. "So I'll be late home."

"Right," Mrs Hope called. "Now, don't be a nuisance if Gran and Grandad are busy."

Mandy was already halfway out the front door. "I won't."

She met James coming across the green. "It's here!" she shouted, even before she reached him. "The egg's hatched."

James's face was brimming with excitement. "When?" he panted. "What's the duckling like? How big is it? What colour? Is it all right?"

Mandy answered all his questions on the way to school. "And I'm calling her Dilly," she finished, as they reached the school gates. "Good, don't you think?"

"Excellent," said James. "I can't wait to see her."

All day, lessons seemed to drag. Mandy felt as though they would never end.

The bell finally rang for home time, and Mandy was first out. She waited impatiently for James by the school gate. When he arrived, they both pedalled like the wind to Lilac Cottage.

When they got there, there was an old blue van in the drive. Gran was just coming out of the greenhouse with a tall grey-haired lady.

Gran introduced her. "This is my friend, Kathy."

"Hello. I'm sorry about your cat," Mandy said, remembering Grandad's conversation with Kathy on the phone.

Gran's friend looked sad. "Thank you, my dear," she replied. "But Snowball had a good, long life. He was eighteen, you know."

"Wow!" James said. "Eighteen. *Twice* as old as you, Mandy. That's *really* old."

Gran and Kathy couldn't help smiling.

"You must really miss her," Mandy said.

"Yes," Kathy replied sadly. "I do."

"Kathy's brought some food for Dilly," Gran said.

"Chick crumbs," Kathy explained.

"Chick crumbs?" James burst out.

"Yes. But they're fine for ducklings too."

"Oh, thank you!" Mandy took the bag gratefully, and she and James went into the greenhouse to see Dilly.

"She's lovely!" James said, as he crouched down and stroked Dilly's downy head.

Dilly was cheeping loudly.

"She must be starving by now," Mandy said. "I'll ask Gran if she's got an old saucer we can put her food on."

Gran and Kathy had gone into the kitchen to make a cup of tea. An old saucer was soon found.

"Let's go and see her have her first dinner," Gran said.

They followed Mandy back to the greenhouse, and Mandy put a handful of chick crumbs on to the saucer, then lifted Dilly carefully out of her box. The little duckling began gobbling them up straight away.

Mandy laughed. "She *was* hungry, wasn't she?"

Full up now with chick crumbs, Dilly settled herself down next to Mandy's feet.

James laughed. "She likes you, Mandy. She's really snuggled up to your shoes."

Behind them, Kathy was smiling broadly. "I bet I know what's happened," she said.

"What?" Mandy and James asked together.

"Were you there when she hatched out?" Kathy asked Mandy.

Mandy shook her head. "No, but I was the first one to see her."

"And she was in your Gran's glass bowl?"

"Yes," Mandy replied, puzzled.

"Well," Kathy said, "I reckon she's imprinted on your shoes."

"*Imprinted?*" James frowned.

Mandy explained quickly what it meant.

Grandad had been listening. He chuckled. "So Dilly thinks Mandy is her mum!"

Gran shook her head. "No, that's not right, Tom," she said with a broad grin. "Dilly thinks Mandy's *shoes* are her mum."

James snorted and burst out laughing.

"It's not funny," Mandy said indignantly. "How would you like a pair of school shoes for a mother?"

6

An argument

Mandy and James stayed with Dilly for a while. Grandad had found a little water dish for her. She had drunk some of the water, dipping in her tiny beak, then putting her head up to swallow it. Mandy thought Dilly was the most adorable creature she had ever seen.

Mandy realised that she was hungry too,

and decided it was time to go home for tea. James agreed. She put Dilly back into her box and put the water beside her. "There you are, Dilly," she said. "Now, be good, won't you?"

They went out, closing the greenhouse door behind them to keep in the warmth. Then they popped their heads round the kitchen door to say goodbye.

"And thanks for the duckling food," Mandy said to Kathy.

"You're welcome, my dear," Kathy replied. She was sitting at the kitchen table with Gran. They were counting out the money they had collected to pay for the guided tour round Woodbridge Farm Park. "But you know she can't live in your grandad's greenhouse forever," she added gently. "She'll need a pen and some water to swim in. And grass and water-weed to peck at."

"That's true," James said.

Mandy sighed. "I know."

"See what your mum and dad think," Gran suggested.

Mandy's heart sank. "Yes," she said, "I will." But she had the feeling she knew exactly what they would say. Animal Ark was too busy to have Dilly around.

Gran must have seen Mandy's crestfallen face. "Don't worry," she said. "We'll fix something. Dilly's all right here for a while." She got up and gave her granddaughter a quick hug.

Mandy and James walked together down to the village green.

"See you tomorrow," James said, as they went their separate ways.

Mandy waved goodbye and set off for home. Her mind was in a whirl. What *was* she going to do with Dilly? Ducklings grew rapidly: they needed to be with other ducks. Maybe she should wait a day or two, then take Dilly back to Millers Pond.

Mandy sighed again as she pushed open the gate to Animal Ark and went up the path. She would just have to talk it over with Mum and Dad. Even if she couldn't

57

keep Dilly at home, they would know what to do.

In the waiting-room, Jean was just putting the cover on her computer ready to go home. Mr Hope was in his surgery. To Mandy's surprise she could hear him arguing with someone. Dad hardly ever raised his voice, or lost his temper. He did get annoyed with people who didn't take proper care of their animals, but he usually managed to keep calm about it. This time, though, seemed to be different.

"It's no good, Mr Taylor," he was saying. "I won't do it and that's that. You'll have to find another solution."

Just then, Mrs Hope came through to check if there were any more patients to be seen.

"Mandy!" she said. "You're back. How's Dilly?"

"She's adorable, Mum. You must go and see her."

"I intend to," replied Mrs Hope. "This evening in fact, if there aren't any emergency calls."

Loud voices were still coming from Mr Hope's surgery. Mrs Hope pulled a face at Jean and shrugged her shoulders.

"What's going on?" Mandy asked.

Her mum shrugged again. "I'm not sure. A man came in with a cat basket, disappeared into the surgery and they've been arguing ever since."

"Mr Taylor," Jean explained. "Lives in one of those new houses ... Orchard Farm Close." She snorted. "Used to be a lovely apple orchard when I was a girl."

"What was wrong with the cat?" Mandy asked.

Jean shook her head. "No idea. Mr Taylor just demanded to see a vet, so I sent him through."

Just then the surgery door flew open. A short, dark, red-faced man wearing a business suit and shiny black shoes came through into the waiting-room.

"Give me the number of the animal sanctuary," he demanded of Jean.

Mandy could just see a small cat inside the basket. Not a kitten, but perhaps about ten months old. A Siamese. She could just see its beautiful, vivid eyes. They looked scared as they peered through the wire mesh at the front of the basket.

"There's no point," Jean said calmly. "Miss Hilder is on holiday and the person looking after things can't take any animals until she gets back."

"And how long will *that* be?" the man snapped. He dumped the basket at his feet and leaned his elbows on the counter. Before Jean could answer, his mobile phone rang. He took it out of his pocket.

"Yes . . . No . . . No. I'm at the vet's and I've got to go back home before I come to work. I'll be about half an hour." He switched off the phone and put it back in his pocket.

"Well?" he said to Jean. "How long will the woman be away?"

"Two weeks," Emily Hope told him.

"Two weeks?" The man suddenly seemed to notice her and Mandy standing there staring at him. He heaved a sharp

sigh. "Right." He picked up the basket, bumping it against the door as he barged through. "I'll find somewhere else," he said over his shoulder.

When he came through into the waiting-room, Mr Hope was red in the face. "That man!" he said angrily.

Mandy desperately wanted to know what they had been arguing about. But she also wanted to tell her dad about Dilly. The news about the duckling came out first. Her words tumbled over one another until Mr Hope had to hold up his hand, a broad grin replacing the angry look on his face.

"Hold your horses, Mandy. Dilly thinks your shoes are *what*?"

"Her mother!" Mandy repeated.

"Well, I think that's really sweet," Jean commented. She put her glasses in her bag and headed towards the door.

"So do I." Mrs Hope smiled. "You saved her life, so you deserve to be her mum."

"You mean, her *shoes* do," Mr Hope said, grinning. He had calmed down, now the man with the cat had left.

"Yes," Mandy said. "But *I'll* be wearing the shoes, so it's up to me to keep her safe. Just as a real mother would do."

"Well, love," Mrs Hope said after tea, when Mandy asked her about finding a proper home for Dilly. "You know we really haven't got time to look after Dilly here."

Mandy did know, of course, but she argued just the same. "One little duckling won't take much looking after," she said.

"No, that's true," Mrs Hope replied. "But someone needs to be here. Dad and I are busy; you're at school. What would Dilly do on her own all day?"

Mandy sighed. "Yes. I know you're right, Mum," she said unhappily. "We'll just have to take her back to Millers Pond, that's all . . . when she's big enough, of course."

Mr Hope had his nose stuck in the *Walton Gazette*. When he heard Mandy mention Millers Pond, he looked up and shook his head. "That's no good, Mandy. She couldn't survive in the wild now; she's too used to human beings. She'll have lost her instinct for survival."

"Anyway," her mum added, "the other ducks might attack her. No, we'll have to find another solution."

Mr Hope had gone back to his paper. "Well, I never!" he suddenly exclaimed. "It's Mr Taylor."

"Mr Taylor?" Emily Hope said with a frown.

"The man with the cat," her husband reminded her.

Mrs Hope peered over her husband's shoulder. "What's he in the paper for?"

Mr Hope read aloud. " 'Paul Taylor, manager of the Walton Shoe Company, has been given the job of setting up a new business in the United States. He and his wife will move to Boston.' " He looked up. "He told me he was leaving Welford. *That's* why he wanted that lovely young Siamese put to sleep."

Mandy's hand flew to her mouth in horror. "Put to sleep!"

"Shocking!" Mrs Hope said. "Why can't he simply find the poor creature another home?"

Mr Hope shook his head. "He didn't think he'd be able to because—"

Just then the phone rang. Mr Hope got up to answer it and came back looking grim. "That was Grandad, Mandy. You'd better get up to Lilac Cottage right away. Dilly's got out of her box and they can't find her anywhere."

7

Where's Dilly?

Heart thudding, Mandy ran out of the house. She grabbed her bike and pedalled furiously to Lilac Cottage. Dilly missing? Where on earth could she have gone?

Her heart turned with fear. If Dilly met a cat . . . The lady next door to Gran and Grandad had a cat . . . a fierce ginger one that was always catching baby birds.

And sometimes a fox would venture on to the village green . . . It didn't bear thinking about.

In the cottage garden, Grandad was on his hands and knees with his head in the shrubbery. All Mandy could see was his bottom and his legs sticking out.

"Dilly, good duck. Come on, where are you?" he called.

Gran was at the other end of the garden, trying to see behind the shed. There was a pile of old flowerpots and plastic seed trays behind there, in which Dilly might be hiding. She was calling too. "Dilly . . . Nice duck . . . Where are you?"

"When did you realise she'd gone?" Mandy gasped.

Grandad backed out of the shrubbery and looked up. "Only a few minutes ago. The greenhouse door was open just a tiny bit. Enough for her to squeeze through." He sat back on his heels. "I'm sorry, Mandy. She's as lively as a monkey, that's for sure."

Mandy turned round and round. Dilly

could be anywhere in the garden. She could even have gone off down the street. Mandy had an awful feeling she knew why Dilly had escaped: she had been looking for Mandy's shoes. Nature told Dilly to follow them wherever they went.

Through the greenhouse glass, Mandy could see Dilly's box. It contained everything she needed . . . except a mother. Mandy bit her lip. She felt guilty. *She* had been the one to rescue Dilly; *she* should have been looking after her, not Gran and Grandad. "Oh, Dilly . . . Where are you?" she murmured. "Please be safe."

"I'll look out in the street," she called, making her way back down the path, looking in between the shrubs and flowers as she went. Then she went through the gate and up and down the road. Surely Dilly couldn't have gone far?

Up and down, up and down the road Mandy trudged. But there was no sign of Dilly anywhere. Mandy went back to Lilac Cottage close to tears.

Grandad had climbed the fence at the back of the garden and gone off towards the allotments.

Gran was sitting on the garden seat looking upset. "I'm so sorry, Mandy," she said. She shook her head. "I went in to peep at Dilly and I must have left the greenhouse door open a tiny bit. What a hopeless gran I am!"

Mandy sat beside her and gave her a hug. "You're a brilliant gran and everyone makes mistakes. Dilly is my duckling . . . I should be the one minding her, not you."

Mandy made up her mind that if they did find Dilly safe and well she would ask Mum and Dad again if she could keep her at Animal Ark. It would only be for a little while, until they found her a new home.

She left Gran and went back into the greenhouse. The box looked so empty without Dilly. There was a little hollow in the straw where the duckling had made herself comfortable.

Mandy had a horrible feeling she might never see Dilly again. She burst into tears.

She was just blowing her nose when she heard a strange sound. A rustle, and a cheep.

She looked down just as a little beak popped out from behind one of Grandad's tomato plants.

Cheep, cheep!

Then Dilly came running out. She had seen Mandy's shoes. In fact, Mandy decided afterwards, they were just what she had been waiting for.

"Gran! Grandad!" Mandy scooped the tiny creature up in her hands. "She's here . . . She's all right. Come and see!"

Grandad came hurrying up the front path. He had gone all the way round the back, through the allotments and out into the road. Mrs Hope was with him. He had met her hurrying up from Animal Ark to see what she could do to help.

"Thank goodness!" Gran touched Dilly's tiny, downy head with her fingertip. Then she looked at Mandy's mum.

Her eyes were shining with tears. "Oh, Emily, I would never have forgiven myself if anything had happened to her."

Mrs Hope was gazing at Dilly. It was the first time she had seen her, and Mandy could tell she was enchanted too.

At last her mum gave a huge sigh. "OK, Mandy," she said, "you win. You're quite right. *You* were the one to rescue Dilly, so *you* should be the one looking after her."

Mandy gave a little cry. "Oh, thanks, Mum. She won't be a nuisance, honestly. And James will help me, I know he will. We'll feed her and clean her out and take her for walks . . ."

Mrs Hope smiled. "I don't think you need to take a duckling for walks, Mandy. Feeding and cleaning will probably be quite enough."

Grandad sorted out a makeshift lid for the box so they could carry Dilly home.

Mandy chatted excitedly as they made their way back to Animal Ark. "She could go in the shed, couldn't she? She'd be quite safe in there. I'll go to the church jumble sale on Saturday and find her an old plastic bowl to swim in."

Mrs Hope smiled again. "Great idea, Mandy. Mind you, she can't stay in the shed forever. She needs fresh air and sunshine. We'll ask your dad to make a little run for her out on the lawn."

At home, Mr Hope said that would be no trouble at all. "In fact," he said to Mandy when Dilly had been put safely in the shed for the night, "I've got some chicken wire somewhere. I'll sort it out tomorrow if I get time."

Mandy hugged him as tight as she could. "Oh thanks, Dad. You're the best dad in the world." She hugged her mum, too. "And you're the best mum."

"What, better than a pair of school shoes?" Mrs Hope asked, with a twinkle in her eye.

Before she went to bed Mandy wrote her *Duckling Diary*. There were so many exciting things to write about that she filled up two whole pages.

★

Next morning, Mandy fed Dilly, cleaned out her box and gave her fresh water and a saucer of chick crumbs. Dilly settled down to eat them, but when Mandy tried to leave she ran cheeping behind her.

"Now stay there," Mandy commanded. She picked her up gently and put her back by her saucer.

When Mandy turned to go again, Dilly was right behind her. Mandy was so charmed she couldn't help letting Dilly follow her into the house so her mum and dad could see. She walked through the garden, up the step and into the kitchen with Dilly right behind her.

Mrs Hope was getting ready for surgery. Mandy danced round the kitchen with Dilly cheeping behind her and flapping her little wings as if she was trying to fly.

Mrs Hope laughed helplessly and Mandy's dad came out of his study to see what all the noise was about.

"I don't know!" He shook his head and grinned broadly. "This place is more

like a zoo than a veterinary practice."

Still laughing, Mandy picked Dilly up gently, and took her back out to the shed. "Sorry, Dilly," she explained, and put her into her box. "Dad will make that pen for you as soon as he can."

She had read in her library book that, in the wild, ducklings were swimming around with their mum within a few days of hatching. The sooner she got that bowl so Dilly had somewhere to swim, the better!

Just then, James turned up. Mandy had phoned him the evening before to tell him Dilly was at Animal Ark. He'd insisted on saying hello to Dilly before they set off for school.

He was just doing so when Mrs Hope called from the kitchen. "I'm off on my calls now, Mandy. Hurry up, or you'll both be late for school."

They said goodbye to Dilly and shut the shed door firmly. Back indoors, Mandy sorted out her school things, grabbed her lunch box, then she and

James set off across the green.

Outside the post office Mrs McFarlane was sweeping the pavement in front of the door. She laughed when she saw Mandy and James. Mandy waved. "Morning, Mrs McFarlane."

"Are you taking your friend to school?" Mrs McFarlane called.

James screwed up his nose. "Does she mean me? I'm quite old enough to go to school by myself, thank you!"

Mandy laughed. "I don't know what she means."

Then Jean Knox pulled up outside the post office and got out of her car.

"Hi, Jean!" Mandy called. "We've got Dilly at home now!"

Jean just stood and stared. "No, you haven't," she called. "You've got her right behind you."

And when Mandy and James turned round, there was Dilly waddling frantically across the green. She was trying desperately to keep up with their strides.

"Oh, no! How did she get out?"

Mandy ran and picked her up, cradling the tiny creature in her hands.

James shook his head. "We made sure the door was shut. There must be a hole in the shed somewhere."

"Oh, dear," Mandy said. "I should have checked. What *are* we going to do with you?" she murmured to the duckling. "I'd better take her back," she said to James.

But just then Mrs Todd drew up in her car. She looked puzzled to see Mandy heading for home instead of school.

Mandy explained. "Dilly followed me," she told her teacher. "You see, she thinks my shoes are her mother."

"Oh . . . I see," Mrs Todd said, although she didn't look as if she understood at all. "Well, seeing as she's here, why don't you bring her into school now? Then everyone can meet her."

Mandy's eyes shone. "Oh, can I?" Everyone in her class knew about Dilly and she had been dying to show her off.

"Just for the morning," Mrs Todd said.

"I'm sure we'll be able to find a box for her in the stockroom. You can take her back home at lunch-time. We've all heard so much about Dilly, everyone will be so pleased to see her."

"Hear that, Dilly?" Mandy said, holding the soft creature against her cheek. "You're the most famous duck in Welford!"

8

James's brilliant idea

Mrs Todd was right. Everyone *was* pleased to see Dilly.

And Mandy was right, too. Dilly was indeed the most famous duck in Welford. In fact, she was quite a star. And when Mandy showed everyone how Dilly followed her shoes wherever she went, they thought it was the funniest thing they had ever seen.

Mrs Todd had phoned Animal Ark to explain that Dilly had escaped. She told Mr and Mrs Hope that Mandy would be bringing her back at lunch-time. James got permission to go with her.

When they got there, the shed door was still firmly shut. And, sure enough, when they checked, there was a hole in the corner of the shed where the wood had rotted away.

"We'd better block it up," James suggested.

They found an old wooden box on a shelf at the back of the shed and wedged it firmly against the hole. While Mandy was feeding Dilly, James checked to see if there were any more holes.

Satisfied at last that Dilly was safe, they settled her in her box and closed the door behind them.

Dilly cheeped madly. Mandy hated leaving her. "She seems so unhappy. I wish I could stay with her all day."

Then James came up with the answer.

"Wear your trainers," he said. "And leave your school shoes here with Dilly. Then she'll be happy."

Mandy's face lit up. "James, what a brilliant idea!"

She ran upstairs to change into her trainers. She knew she wasn't really supposed to wear them to school, but hoped Mrs Todd wouldn't mind. After all, Dilly's happiness was at stake.

Mr and Mrs Hope had come in from work to grab a sandwich for lunch. Her mum spotted the trainers at once. "Mandy, where are your school shoes?" she asked with a frown.

Mandy explained.

"Well," her mum said with a sigh, "I don't suppose it will hurt to wear your trainers for a day or two. And you need new school shoes anyway. We'll try to get to Walton at the weekend to buy you some."

"So it's OK to leave my shoes with Dilly? Oh, thanks, Mum!" Mandy gave her a hug. "I knew you'd understand."

Mandy and James ran out to the shed.

"Here you are, Dilly." Mandy put her shoes into the box. Dilly gave a cheep, fluffed out her feathers and settled down, looking as happy as could be.

"There you are," James said. "What did I tell you?"

"You *are* a genius, James," Mandy said.

When Mandy arrived home from school that afternoon there was a message from Grandad. They had found an old plastic baby bath that Dilly could have as a swimming-pool. Grandad had used it to wash his flowerpots in, but he had cleaned it up for Dilly. Mandy wouldn't have to wait for the jumble sale after all.

There was another surprise as well. Mr Hope had found time to make Dilly's run. He had also made a little house from another wooden box he had found at the back of the shed.

"That's great, Dad." Mandy's eyes shone when she saw it. "Dilly's going to love it."

Mr Hope grinned, although he shook his head at the same time. "We don't want her to love it *too* much, Mandy. We have to find her somewhere to go where she can be with other ducks," he explained.

Mandy's face fell. "I know, Dad. I've been thinking about it for ages."

Mr Hope put his arm across her shoulders. "Well, try not to worry, love. We'll find somewhere."

Mandy racked her brains as she carried

Dilly to her new pen. The trouble was, she couldn't think of *anywhere*.

Dilly seemed delighted with her new house and run. She ran around cheeping and pecking at the grass. Then she ran into her little house and ran out again. Mandy and James had planned to go to Millers Pond later to get some waterweed to put in her bath.

Mandy gazed at her dad. "She loves it, Dad. Thanks."

Mandy placed her shoes next to Dilly's house and stood up with a sigh. There was just time to write in her diary and go to Lilac Cottage before tea.

She went upstairs to her room, took her diary from her desk and began to write. The pages were almost filled up. She wrote about how Dilly had followed her to school, and how much everyone had loved her. She drew a little picture of Dilly in her pen, sitting with Mandy's shoes.

When she turned over, she realised that there was only one page left and it would soon be time to take the diary to school to show Mrs Todd. It made her feel sad. The last entry would have to be Dilly's new home. She bit her lip. If *only* she could think of somewhere where Dilly would be safe and happy.

Mandy sighed, put her diary away and went downstairs. She popped her head round the surgery door to tell her mum she was off to Lilac Cottage.

"Cheer up, Mandy," Mrs Hope said. "Dilly's OK, isn't she?"

Mandy sighed again. "Yes, she's fine."

"That's good, then," her mum said.

On her way to her grandparents', several people stopped to ask how Dilly was. It seemed Dilly's fame had spread even wider.

"She's fine," Mandy told Mr Hadcroft, the vicar. "But I've got to find her a new home soon. She needs to be with other ducks."

Mr Hadcroft looked thoughtful. "If I hear of anyone who can provide a suitable home for her, I'll definitely let you know," he said.

Another man came walking down the road. Mandy recognised him at once. It was Mr Taylor, the man who had wanted his cat put to sleep. He was hurrying towards the post office with a bundle of letters in his hand.

"Hello, Mr Taylor," Mandy said. She just *had* to find out what had happened to his cat.

Mr Taylor stopped, frowning. He was red in the face and obviously in a hurry. "Do I know you, young lady?"

Mandy told him who she was, and when he heard she was the vet's daughter he looked a bit sheepish. "Oh," he said. "Well, I still haven't done anything about LaLa."

"*LaLa?*" It was the strangest name for a cat Mandy had ever heard.

"We called her that because when she miaows she sounds as if she's singing," he explained. He sighed. "I know my wife's going to be really upset, but it seems the kindest thing."

"Why?" Mandy asked indignantly.

"LaLa's not sick, is she?"

Mr Taylor frowned. "Didn't your father tell you?"

Mandy shook her head. "No."

"She's deaf, poor thing. I really didn't think anyone would want her and we just can't take her to America with us." He waved his hand and hurried away. "Sorry, young lady, I must go to catch the post."

Mandy stared after him. Deaf? Well, that wasn't the end of the world. Mr

Taylor just hadn't tried hard enough, that was all. Poor LaLa!

She ran on to Lilac Cottage. She couldn't wait to get the baby bath for Dilly to swim in.

Grandad was in his workshop fixing a broken chair. Gran was on her outing to Woodbridge Farm Park.

"It's in the kitchen," Grandad told Mandy when she asked about the baby bath. "Good as new, and waiting for you."

"Thanks, Grandad," Mandy said and ran indoors to fetch it.

She took the bath home to Animal Ark and filled it with water. Dilly cheeped so loudly when Mandy lifted her up to see it that Mandy thought the little creature might burst.

The sides were too high for Dilly to climb in and out, so Mandy found a piece of wood to make a ramp and soon Dilly was swimming happily around. She ducked and dived, splashing her feathers. Then she began preening herself. Mandy knew from her library book that this would begin to make her feathers water-proof. "Oiling up" it was called. Ducks had to do it, otherwise their feathers would soak up the water and they would sink.

After tea Mandy just had time to write in her diary about Dilly and her new bath before James arrived with Blackie. They played with Dilly for a while, then Mandy found a couple of empty jam jars to fill with waterweed. They put on their wellies and set off for Millers Pond.

"Be careful," Mrs Hope called as they went out.

"We will," they replied.

"Dilly's got to learn how to peck at waterweed," Mandy said, as they went along the high street. "Ready for when we find her a *proper* pond to live on."

They made their way up the lane and round the edge of the field that led to the pond. A bird was warbling in the willow tree and dragonflies whirred and flitted to and fro over the surface like bright little helicopters. A couple of moorhens were exploring the long grass. They ran away and splashed into the water when Mandy and James arrived.

They tied Blackie to a tree in case he decided to start chasing things, and went to the shallow end of the pond. They scooped up handfuls of waterweed. One or two pond snails were stuck to the trailing roots, so Mandy carefully picked them off and put them back into the water.

They had filled both jam jars when James suddenly whispered, "Hey . . . look!"

Mandy looked up and saw a dark-brown duck emerging from the over-hanging willow. Behind her swam four ducklings — three dark ones and one a pale, downy yellow.

Mandy drew in her breath. "Oh, aren't they gorgeous?"

"There must have been another nest," James said. "If it was a fox that destroyed

Dilly's nest, at least it didn't find this one."

"Thank goodness," Mandy said.

They watched the little family for a while, then crept quietly away.

"That's what Dilly should be doing," Mandy said sadly as they made their way home. "Swimming around with her mum and brothers and sisters."

"I know." James felt sad as well.

"Not splashing around in an old baby bath," Mandy added.

James sighed. "It's a pity we can't bring her back here."

"I know," Mandy said. "But I'm sure Dad's right. She's too used to humans to survive in the wild now. We've just got to find her somewhere with other ducks, but where there are humans too. The trouble is, I just can't think of anywhere."

"No," James said, looking glum. "Nor can I."

9

A problem solved?

Back home, Mandy put one jam jar full of waterweed into Dilly's bath, keeping the other jar of weed for the next day.

When Dilly went up her little ramp and jumped into the water, Mandy pecked at the weed with her finger to show the duckling what to do. Dilly soon got the idea – she gobbled it up as if it was the most delicious meal ever.

"It'll do her good to get wild food," Mandy said. "She can't live on chick crumbs forever."

When Dilly had finished, they put her away safely in her little house for the night.

"I'll walk home with you if you like," Mandy said to James. "Then we can pop in to thank Gran for the bath on the way."

Mandy and James made their way towards Lilac Cottage. Mrs Ponsonby was sitting on the seat on the village green enjoying the evening sunshine. Pandora, her overweight Pekinese, was sitting beside her.

"Ah . . ." She got up when she saw Mandy and James and came steaming towards them. The feather in her hat waved in the breeze. Pandora waddled beside her, her tail waving like a flag. "How's that little pet of yours? Lilly, is it?" She was a little out of breath as she spoke.

"Dilly," Mandy smiled. "She's fine, thank you."

Mrs Ponsonby sniffed. "I like ducks. I wanted to go on that WI outing today, but they wouldn't allow me to take Pandora to the farm . . . Would they, darling?" she said to the dog, who sat panting at her feet. "How silly," Mrs Ponsonby went on. "She wouldn't have chased anything, would you, sweetheart?"

Pandora made a strange noise – a cross

between a snuffle and a sneeze. It sounded exactly like the word "no".

When they were out of earshot, Mandy couldn't help giggling. "I can't imagine Pandora chasing anything, can you? She's far too unfit."

James shook his head. "Only a chocolate biscuit if you threw it for her."

Mandy laughed again as they walked on to Lilac Cottage.

Kathy's van was parked outside. She and Gran had just arrived back from their trip to the farm park. They were sitting at the kitchen table drinking mugs of tea and looking at some leaflets.

"Did you have a nice time at the farm?" Mandy and James asked as soon as they arrived and had thanked Gran for the baby bath.

"Oh, it was wonderful," Gran said. "Wasn't it, Kathy?"

"It really was," Kathy agreed. "They've got a lovely herd of Jersey cows."

"I love Jerseys," James said.

"We saw them being milked," Kathy

told them. "It's all done by computer nowadays, you know. All the dairyman does is press buttons."

"Wow!" James said.

"They keep sheep too," Gran said. "And goats. Even a llama."

"A llama?" Mandy exclaimed. "How brilliant!"

"He was very friendly," Gran said. "People breed them for their lovely wool, you know, although this one was more like a pet."

"What else have they got?" Mandy asked.

Gran got up to fetch the lemonade and biscuits. "A pets corner, with rabbits, gerbils and guinea-pigs," she told them.

Mandy sighed. "I'd love to go and see them."

"Didn't Grandad promise to take you?" Gran said, as she put two glasses of lemonade and the biscuit tin in front of them.

"Yes," Mandy said.

"Well then, he will," Gran reassured her.

Kathy was still reading one of the brochures. On the front was a picture. It showed a wooden sign spelling out "Woodbridge Farm Park". Behind the sign was a lake with a willow tree.

Mandy stared. Then she pointed to the picture. "Did you see any wild ducks on this lake?" she asked, excitedly.

"Yes. They come to feed with the farm ducks, but they're used to human beings and are very tame," Kathy replied.

Gran suddenly seemed to realise what Mandy was getting at. And so did Kathy. A broad smile spread across her face. "Oh, Mandy, that would be the perfect place for Dilly!"

Mandy drew in her breath. "Do you think they would take her?"

Gran picked up another brochure, and found a phone number. "There's never any harm in asking," she said. "You don't get anywhere unless you ask." She handed the leaflet to Mandy. "There's the number. Why don't you phone them?"

Mandy went out into the hall and dialled the number. But there was no reply.

Gran patted her shoulder. "I expect they're busy outside with the animals. Try again later."

Mandy sat down at the table and put her chin on her hands. "If they do take Dilly," she said, "I'll miss her like anything."

"Yes, love," Gran said. "But you know you can't keep her much longer."

"I know." Mandy sighed again.

"That's the trouble with having pets," Kathy said. "You miss them so much when they've gone." She had a little catch in her voice. Mandy knew she was talking about her cat, Snowball.

"You could get another cat," James said.

"It's really rather difficult," Kathy tried to explain. "Especially with all my chicks. Snowball was a rather special cat as he was deaf, you see."

"Yes . . ." Mandy said slowly. An idea

was coming into her head. A brilliant
idea! Mr Taylor's cat was special too. So
special that Mr Taylor didn't think anyone would want her. But Mandy knew
someone who would want her *because* she
was deaf. LaLa wouldn't hear chicks
cheeping and try to chase them. She was
the perfect new pet for Kathy.

She jumped out of her chair suddenly.
"Gran, may I use the phone again?"

Gran looked a bit startled. "Yes, of
course, love. But the people at the farm

will probably still be busy."

"No, I need to ask Dad something," Mandy said.

"Well," Kathy got up as well, "I've got to go and feed my hens."

"No, please wait a minute," Mandy said. "Please wait."

She ran out into the hall and dialled Animal Ark's number. If her dad had Mr Taylor's address, she knew he would give it to her. And she also *knew* that Mr Taylor would gladly give LaLa to Kathy.

But, as she waited impatiently for someone to answer, her heart suddenly sank. Mr Taylor had been desperate to get rid of his cat. What if it was already too late?

10

Another problem solved?

Mandy waited impatiently for someone at Animal Ark to answer the phone. She was just about to give up when she heard her mum's voice.

She explained breathlessly what she wanted.

"Hang on," her mum said. "I'll go and ask Dad."

She soon came back with Mr Taylor's address and phone number.

Mandy scribbled down the details on the notepad by the phone. "Thanks, Mum."

"But why do you want it?" her mum asked.

"I'll tell you later. Bye!" Mandy put down the phone and ran back into the kitchen. But, to her disappointment, Kathy had gone.

"She couldn't wait," Gran explained. "She said the hens would be starving."

"Let's see if we can catch her, James," Mandy said.

They rushed outside.

Luckily Kathy was still at the gate. Grandad had come back from visiting his friend and she was telling him about their trip.

Kathy listened carefully as Mandy told her about Mr Taylor and LaLa. At first she was unsure that she wanted to replace Snowball so soon after he'd died. But when Mandy came to the bit about Mr

Taylor wanting the Siamese put to sleep, Kathy's hand flew to her mouth. "What a horrible man! Where did you say he lived?"

"Here." Mandy thrust the bit of paper in front of her.

"Right," Kathy said. "It's on my way home. I think I'll pay him a visit. Would you like to come, you two? And Blackie, of course?"

"Yes, please!" they said together.

"I'll phone your mum to tell her where you've gone," Grandad said to Mandy.

"Could you tell mine as well, please?" James asked.

Grandad promised he would. They climbed into Kathy's van and set off.

The Taylors' house was one of four big new houses in a small close at the end of the village. It had a long path leading up to an oak front door.

"Oh, dear," Kathy said as they drew up outside. "It looks as if they've gone."

They stared at the house. There were no curtains at the windows, and the garage was empty. The whole place looked deserted.

"They can't have," Mandy wailed. "I only saw Mr Taylor yesterday."

Then a thin lady wearing jeans and a T-shirt came from round the back of the house with two black sacks full of rubbish. She walked up the path and dumped them outside the front gate.

They all got out of the car.

"Mrs Taylor?" Kathy asked.

The woman nodded.

Kathy told her who they were.

"And we wanted to know if you've still got LaLa," Mandy blurted out, before she could stop herself.

"Yes," Kathy added. "Because I'd like to give her a home."

"Oh, *would* you?" Mrs Taylor looked as if she was going to burst into tears. "I was so angry with my husband for taking her to see Mr Hope. He said he just didn't know what else to do. You do know that she's—"

"Yes," Kathy said quickly. She then told Mrs Taylor about Snowball and the chicks. "So, you see, she'll suit me perfectly," she said.

Five minutes later, LaLa was safely installed on the back seat of Kathy's van in her carrying basket.

LaLa stared at them with her huge, sky-blue eyes. Mandy poked her finger through the wire mesh and touched her silky head. "Don't worry, LaLa," she said. "You'll be OK now."

"She's very nervous," Mrs Taylor said, as she thanked them again.

"Don't worry," Kathy assured her. "With gentle handling and a lot of tender loving care I'm sure she'll soon settle down."

She said thanks to Mrs Taylor again and turned on the ignition. "I'll run you two back. I can make an appointment for LaLa to have a check-up at the same time."

At Animal Ark, Mr and Mrs Hope were delighted to hear the good news.

"Bring her in in the morning," Mr Hope said to Kathy as she deposited Mandy at the front door. "I'll give her a good going-over."

Mandy waved as Kathy hurried off to feed her hens and drop James home. Then Mandy turned to her dad and told him about their plan for Dilly.

He smiled. "That's a great idea, Mandy."

"If they'll take her," she said.

"Let's try and ring again," said Mr Hope. "Then we'll know one way or the other."

"Right," Mandy agreed.

This time someone did answer. It was the farm manager, and Mandy suddenly felt tongue-tied. It was a bit of a long story. And would he understand about her shoes?

"Dad," she said, when she had told the man at the other end who she was. "Could you explain – please?"

Five minutes later, Mr Hope put the phone down. He had a broad grin on his face. "They'll be glad to have her," he said. "Tomorrow's Saturday. We'll take her after morning surgery. OK?"

Mandy threw her arms around him. "Oh, Dad, that's great!"

"Mind you," Mr Hope warned, "he said the other ducks might give her a bit of a hard time at first."

"Dilly's very brave," Mandy insisted. "She'll stick up for herself."

"Well, I hope so," Mr Hope said. "And she'll miss your shoes, Mandy."

"I could leave them there," Mandy said.

Mr Hope looked dubious. "I don't

know how. If you leave them on the bank, she might not want to swim. If you put them in the water, they'll sink."

"Oh, dear." Mandy felt crestfallen. Dad was right. She wanted Dilly to have a proper home, other ducks to play with and proper food to eat. But she didn't want her to be miserable.

She suddenly had an idea. Maybe Grandad could help.

Mandy went to phone her grandad. Grandad listened carefully to what she had to say. Then he said, "OK, Mandy. I'll see what I can do."

Mandy felt close to tears as she made the next to last entry in her *Duckling Diary*. She knew she would hate saying good-bye. But there were some things you just had to do. Some bridges you had to cross.

Before bed, she went to take a peep at Dilly. The duckling was fast asleep, tucked up in her little house with one of Mandy's shoes. She opened one eye and gave a cheep as Mandy carefully lifted the lid to look at her.

Mandy touched the downy head with her finger. Dilly was growing so fast. She would quickly lose her baby feathers, and it wouldn't be long before she stopped cheeping and started to quack. In fact, she would soon be quite grown up.

Mandy wiped away a tear, closed the lid softly and went back indoors.

Next morning, Grandad and James arrived at the same time, just as the last patient left the surgery. Mandy rushed out to greet them. "Grandad, you've done it!" she cried, looking at the object he carried under his arm.

"Yes." Grandad showed her. It was a little raft made from two short pieces of wood nailed together. Underneath, he had fixed two pieces of polystyrene foam that would help the wood to stay afloat.

James frowned. "What on earth is it?"

"It's a raft," Mandy explained. "Grandad made it. We're going to float my shoes on it, so Dilly will have them with her for as long as she wants."

Mandy's mum and dad looked amazed when they saw it.

"Whose idea was *that*?" Mr Hope asked.

"Mine, of course," Mandy replied.

"I'm not sure it'll work . . ." Mrs Hope began.

Mandy looked indignant. "It will," she said. "I just know it."

Grandad took some string from his pocket and Mandy tied the shoes firmly to the raft. "There," she said. "That should do the trick." Now all they had to do was fetch Dilly.

Mandy felt sad as she lifted the little duckling gently from her baby bath. She put her into the box that she had lived in at Lilac Cottage and carried her out to the front, where the others were waiting.

They set off along the high street. Grandad carried the raft and Mandy had Dilly's box safely tucked under her arm.

The farm was on the Walton road, just outside the village. When they arrived,

Mr Marsh, the farm manager, came out
to greet them.

He shook hands with everyone and
took a peep at Dilly. "She's great," he
said. "She looks very healthy." He turned
to Mandy. "You've done a good job
there, Mandy."

"And James," Mandy said quickly.
"She's *his* duckling, as well."

"Well done, the pair of you, then," Mr
Marsh said. "Right, let's go, shall we?"
Then he noticed the raft with the shoes
attached to it. "What's on earth's that for?"

He laughed when Mandy explained.

"It'll be all right, won't it?" she asked anxiously. "It won't scare the other ducks?"

"I shouldn't think so," Mr Marsh assured her. "Come on, let's find out."

The lake was in the field behind the hay barn, and was shaped like a fat figure of eight, with a weeping willow at one end. The edges were lined with bulrushes and huge yellow irises. On it, ducks and geese of all varieties were swimming around.

"We're really pleased the wild ducks come here to feed," Mr Marsh said. "They mix very well with our own."

Dotted here and there were little duck houses with ramps going down into the water.

"They're safe from predators," Mr Marsh explained. "Foxes will swim a little way to raid nests, but not that far."

"We know," Mandy said sadly. "We think that's what happened to Dilly's brothers and sisters."

Mr Marsh patted her shoulder. "Don't worry," he said. "She'll be safe here."

There were several families of ducks swimming in and out of the rushes. One came towards them as they stood by the edge.

"That little family are about the same age." Mr Marsh pointed to them. "Hopefully she'll tag along with them."

Everyone held their breath as Mandy bent down and put the raft into the water.

"I'm not at all sure this is going to work," Grandad said, biting his lip. Then his face broke into a broad grin as the raft, plus shoes, floated perfectly. "There you are," he said. "I knew it would."

"Oh, Dad!" Mrs Hope said, laughing.

Grandad winked at her and laughed too.

Mandy opened the box and took Dilly out. The duckling sat in her hands, cheeping. Then she seemed to smell the water and the fresh air, because she raised her beak to the breeze and gave the loudest cheep she had ever given.

"You'd better put her in," Mrs Hope suggested gently. "The sooner the others see her, the better."

Mandy crouched down and spread her hands out over the surface of the water. Dilly took one look, then jumped in with a little splash. She saw the raft and swam swiftly towards it, her little head bobbing to and fro.

The other gang of ducklings began swimming towards her. As they closed in on Dilly, Mandy held her breath. Her heart seemed to be beating right up in her throat. "Please be all right," she whispered. "Please be all right."

She felt her mother's arm go round her shoulders.

One of the ducklings – the biggest – suddenly flew at Dilly, cheeping. There was a swift flurry, a blur of ducklings and splashing water. Then the others came closer to get a better view of what was going on.

"Oh . . . no," Mandy gasped, "they're going to hurt her."

But Dilly was much too brave for that. She swam away, then turned quickly and pecked the bigger duckling smartly on the tail. She turned and swam back rapidly towards the little raft, and the other duckling followed her. The others arrived and suddenly there was another flurry. It seemed the water was boiling with squabbling ducklings.

Then Dilly emerged. She swam round in circles, with the others behind her. They seemed to lose interest then and swam away to where the mother duck was waiting for them. Dilly clambered up on to the raft, shook herself, and stood there beside Mandy's shoes, just watching the others.

On the bank, Mandy clasped her mother's hand tightly. Dilly *had* to go and swim with the others. It was great to have the shoes there, but she couldn't stay with them forever.

Suddenly, Dilly gave a loud cheep and plunged into the water. She swam as fast as she could towards the other ducklings.

They turned and stared at her. Then, as they swam away towards the other side of the pond, Dilly followed them. Soon all five ducklings were playing together, splashing and diving as if they were already the best of friends.

"Bye, Dilly," Mandy whispered, as everyone clapped and cheered. "Have a lovely time."

Her eyes were shining as she turned to James. "Wasn't she brave?"

"Yes," James agreed. "Brave and brilliant."

They watched as Dilly and her new family disappeared into the reeds.

"She'll be fine," Mr Marsh said with a sigh of relief. "Absolutely fine."

"I think she's gone off my shoes already," Mandy said. She turned to her grandad. "I'm sorry. Maybe you didn't need to make the raft after all."

Grandad gave her a hug. "It's OK, Mandy. As long as Dilly is all right, then nothing else matters."

As they made their way back to the

village Mandy knew what Grandad said was true. "Well," she said, with a sigh. "At least my *Duckling Diary* will have a happy ending."

When they got back home James went off to get Blackie, and Mandy went to her room to write the very last page of her diary. She sighed as she wrote down the morning's events, and felt sad as she carefully drew a picture of the raft with her shoes attached to it and Dilly swimming away to join her new friends.

"I was so proud of Dilly as she went off to play with her new duckling friends," she wrote. "Now I know she will be safe and happy. This is the end of my *Duckling Diary*."

Mandy quickly read what she had written and then closed the book with a sigh. She ran downstairs and out into the sunshine. It had been great looking after Dilly, but knowing the little duckling was in the best place she could possibly be was easily the nicest feeling of all.

LAMB LESSONS

Lucy Daniels

Mandy Hope loves animals and knows lots about them too – both her parents are vets! So Mandy's always able to help her friends with their pet problems . . .

Mandy's class is doing a project at a local working farm. But she's been paired to work with Dillon, the school bully! Mandy's worried about how he'll treat the animals – especially a tiny lamb called Snowy . . . Perhaps it's time for Dillon to be taught a lesson . . .

LUCY DANIELS

Animal Ark Pets

0 340 67283 8	Puppy Puzzle	£2.99	❏
0 340 67284 6	Kitten Crowd	£2.99	❏
0 340 67285 4	Rabbit Race	£2.99	❏
0 340 67286 2	Hamster Hotel	£2.99	❏
0 340 68729 0	Mouse Magic	£2.99	❏
0 340 68730 4	Chick Challenge	£2.99	❏
0 340 68731 2	Pony Parade	£2.99	❏
0 340 68732 0	Guinea-pig Gang	£2.99	❏
0 340 71371 2	Gerbil Genius	£2.99	❏
0 340 71372 0	Duckling Diary	£2.99	❏

All Hodder Children's books are available at your local bookshop, or can be ordered direct from the publisher. Just tick the titles you would like and complete the details below. Prices and availability are subject to change without prior notice.

Please enclose a cheque or postal order made payable to *Bookpoint Ltd*, and send to: Hodder Children's Books, 39 Milton Park, Abingdon, OXON OX14 4TD, UK.
Email Address: orders@bookpoint.co.uk

If you would prefer to pay by credit card, our call centre team would be delighted to take your order by telephone. Our direct line *01235 400414* (lines open 9.00 am–6.00 pm Monday to Saturday, 24 hour message answering service). Alternatively you can send a fax on *01235 500454*.

TITLE		FIRST NAME		SURNAME	

ADDRESS	

DAYTIME TEL:		POST CODE	

If you would prefer to pay by credit card, please complete:
Please debit my Visa/Access/Diner's Card/American Express (delete as applicable) card no:

Signature .... Expiry Date: ....

If you would NOT like to receive further information on our products please tick the box. ❏